THOMAS & FRIENDS™

THOMAS IN CHARGE

Random House  New York

Thomas the Tank Engine & Friends™
CREATED BY BRITT ALLCROFT
Based on The Railway Series by The Reverend W Awdry.
© 2012 Gullane (Thomas) LLC.
Thomas the Tank Engine & Friends and Thomas & Friends are trademarks of Gullane (Thomas) Limited.
HIT and the HIT Entertainment logo are trademarks of HIT Entertainment Limited.
All rights reserved. Published in the United States by Random House Children's Books, a division of Random House, Inc.,
1745 Broadway, New York, NY 10019, and in Canada by Random House of Canada Limited, Toronto. Random House
and the colophon are registered trademarks of Random House, Inc.
randomhouse.com/kids   www.thomasandfriends.com
ISBN: 978-0-307-93119-1
MANUFACTURED IN CHINA   10 9 8 7 6 5 4 3 2 1

HiT entertainment

It was a beautiful morning on the Island of Sodor. All the engines were busy.

Thomas was puffing to Brendam Docks to shunt coal cars.

Gordon was waiting with the Express.

"Good morning, Gordon!" Thomas said.

"Good morning, Thomas," answered Gordon.

"I'm going to shunt these coal cars faster than fast!" said Thomas.

Gordon was happy that *he* didn't have to shunt coal cars.

"I'm waiting for Sir Topham Hatt," he declared.

Just then, Sir Topham Hatt arrived.

"Today is an important day," he announced. "I am going to meet the Railway Inspector at Knapford Station. Then I will take him on a tour of the Island. Our tour will end here, at the Docks."

Thomas' boiler bubbled. The Railway Inspector was a very important visitor.

"Thomas, I want you to be busy shunting cars while the inspector is here," Sir Topham Hatt instructed. "Busy engines will please him most of all!"

"Bubbling boilers! I must make sure I stay busier than ever!" exclaimed Thomas.

He puffed over to the cars. *"Shunting cars, I do it best; I biff and bash and never rest!"* he peeped.

Suddenly, Thomas stopped. An idea flew into his funnel.

"I must find more engines to shunt cars with me. Then the Railway Inspector will be really pleased. And Sir Topham Hatt will be proud!"

So Thomas left the coal cars and huffed happily out of the Docks.

Thomas puffed into Maron Station. Percy was waiting for his mail cars to be loaded.

"Good morning, Percy!" Thomas called. "I have some important news: the Railway Inspector is coming to Brendam Docks. Sir Topham Hatt said it will make the inspector very pleased to see busy engines shunting there. Will you come?"

"I can't, Thomas," the little green engine said. "I have to deliver the mail."

"But shunting cars will please the inspector most of all," Thomas pointed out. "And it will make Sir Topham Hatt proud."

Percy *wheesh*ed and *whoosh*ed.
"All right, Thomas," he said. "I'll come with you."
And Percy was uncoupled from his mail cars.

Percy puffed away with Thomas—just as the Railway Inspector arrived at Maron Station with Sir Topham Hatt. They had come to see Percy busy with his mail cars. But the station was very quiet. And Percy was nowhere to be seen. . . .

Thomas and Percy huffed happily into the Quarry, where they saw Mavis.

"The Railway Inspector is coming to Brendam Docks," Thomas told Mavis. "Sir Topham Hatt said it will make the inspector very pleased to see busy engines shunting there. Will you come?"

Mavis wasn't sure. "I don't think I can, Thomas," she said. "I have a lot to do here."

"Shunting cars will please the inspector most of all," said Thomas, "and it will make Sir Topham Hatt proud."

Mavis wanted to make Sir Topham Hatt proud.

"All right, Thomas," she said. "I'll come with you!"

So Mavis left her slate cars and clattered away with Thomas—just as Sir Topham Hatt and the Railway Inspector arrived at the Quarry. They had come to see Mavis at work. But the Quarry wasn't busy—it was very, very quiet. The Railway Inspector sighed. And Sir Topham Hatt couldn't believe his eyes.

Thomas puffed back to the Docks. Percy and Mavis were there. They had shunted a long line of cars. Thomas was pleased! Then he heard Gordon puffing down the track.

Poop! Poop!

"Gordon is bringing Sir Topham Hatt and the Railway Inspector!" cried Thomas.

"Quick, Percy! Hurry, Mavis! We must be as busy as bees! The Railway Inspector must be pleased. And Sir Topham Hatt must be proud!"

"One, two, three, push!" yelled Thomas.
Percy shoved. Mavis shunted. But then there was trouble!
The coal cars bashed and biffed together. They juddered and jittered.
Coal dust scattered and splattered everywhere!

The Railway Inspector and Sir Topham Hatt had just arrived—and they got covered in coal dust. It even flew down Gordon's funnel!

Sir Topham Hatt was cross.

"Thomas!" he said. "What have you done?" Thomas felt terrible.

"The Railway Inspector isn't pleased," said Thomas sadly. "Sir Topham Hatt isn't proud. Gordon can't whoosh. And it's all my fault."

Thomas knew he had to chuff and puff to put things right.

"Sir, I will shunt Gordon to the Steamworks," said Thomas. "Victor will make sure his funnel is free and his firebox fizzles. Then Gordon can take you and the Railway Inspector on the tour of Sodor. And I can finally be Really Useful."

Sir Topham Hatt was happy to hear this.

"Very well, Thomas," he said.

So Thomas heaved and hauled his hardest and shunted Gordon away from the Docks.

At the Steamworks, Victor was happy to welcome Gordon and Thomas.
"Well, Thomas, my friend, what have we here?" asked Victor.
"Gordon's funnel is blocked with coal dust," said Thomas. "He needs a clear funnel and a fizzling firebox."
"Then he has come to the right place," said Victor. Soon Gordon's funnel was fixed. His firebox was fiery. And he was ready to take Sir Topham Hatt and the Railway Inspector on a tour of the Island—to see all the Really Useful and very busy engines on Sodor.

Thomas steamed swiftly back to the Docks. He knew he had a lot of work to do!

At the Docks, Thomas shunted and shoved. He huffed his hardest. *"Shunting cars, I do it best; I biff and bash and never rest,"* he sang.

Thomas didn't see Sir Topham Hatt and the Railway Inspector arrive.

"Thomas, you are a Really Useful Engine," said Sir Topham Hatt. "I am very proud of you."

"And I am very pleased to see such a busy engine," said the Railway Inspector. "I wasn't sure before, but now I know that Sir Topham Hatt's railway is the best!"

Thomas beamed and gleamed.

Soon all the engines were fixed. They were ready to be Really Useful again.

"Well done, my friend," said Victor. "Time to go home."

"Not quite, Victor," said Thomas. "It's time to say thank you to Kevin."

"Any time, boss," said Kevin. "I mean, Thomas!"

And everyone laughed and laughed.

Next, Victor and Thomas talked to Henry.

"Don't worry, Henry!" said Thomas. "Your firebox will be cleaned. You won't wheeze and sneeze anymore." And Thomas was right!

Then Victor and Thomas listened to James.

"I don't need a new funnel," said James. "I need my old funnel cleaned and polished!"

"James, you will have the most perfectly polished funnel on Sodor!" promised Thomas.

First, Victor and Thomas went to Spencer.

"I don't need checking from wheels to whistle," said Spencer. "I need new paint for my scuffs and scratches!"

This time, Thomas listened.

"Don't worry, Spencer," he said. "You'll be sparkling silver in no time!" That made Spencer very happy.

Thomas looked at Victor and then at the mess and the muddle.

"Cinders and ashes!" he exclaimed. "This is all my fault! I didn't listen to Victor. I didn't listen to Kevin, and I didn't listen to my friends. I was too excited—and too stubborn!"

"I think, my friend, that you are right," said Victor. "What will you do now?"

"I'm sorry," said Thomas. "Now I will listen to you. And I'll make sure that all the engines are fixed properly."

James was so upset, he blew the biggest puff of steam he had ever blown—all over Victor! Victor had just arrived from the Transfer Yards. Now he was covered from buffer to buffer in twigs, soot, and straw! Victor's wheels wobbled and his steam spluttered.

"Sizzling Sodor!" he exclaimed. "What has happened to my beautiful Steamworks?"

Then Kevin dropped Henry's coal—right in front of Henry's nose!

"Bust my boiler and crashing coals!" cried Kevin. He rocked and rolled straight into James!

"Mind my shiny red paintwork!" exclaimed James.

Then there was trouble! Kevin reeled
and rolled back toward the hoist. And
with a biff and a bash, he hit a big
green button that made Spencer jump
into the air!

"Trembling tracks!" exclaimed
Spencer. "What's happening?"

"Heaving hooks!" Kevin gasped.
"Sorry, Spencer!"

Kevin was now very confused. To find a new funnel for James, he had to put down Henry's coal. But first he had to raise Spencer on the hoist. It was all too much.

"Oh dear, boss—Thomas," he said.

"Don't worry, Kevin," Thomas said. "I'm in charge."

James steamed snootily in. Straw and twigs were blocking his funnel!

"Why are you here, Thomas?" asked James.

"Victor is away today. I'm in charge!" said Thomas. "Bubbling boilers, you *are* in trouble. What happened to you?"

"I can't puff properly," James told him.

"I know just what you need," said Thomas. "Kevin!"

"Yes, boss?" said Kevin. "I mean, Thomas."

"James needs a new funnel," Thomas instructed Kevin.

"No I don't!" cried James.

But Thomas wasn't listening.

"Don't worry, Henry," he said. "We'll have you puffing proudly in no time. Kevin, bring over some of Henry's special coal, please!"

"But . . . but what about Spencer, boss?" asked Kevin.

Thomas wasn't listening.

"Quick as you can, Kevin!" he said.

Then Henry chuffed in. He wasn't well.

"What are you doing here, Thomas?" he asked.

"Victor is away today," said Thomas. "I'm in charge!"

Henry sighed. Then he sneezed and wheezed.

"Footplates and fenders! I know what's wrong with you, Henry!" exclaimed Thomas. "You have been given the wrong coal!"

"No, Thomas," protested Henry. "It's not my . . ."

Soon Spencer steamed sulkily into the Steamworks. His shiny silver paintwork was scratched and scuffed.

"Where's Victor?" he asked.

"He's away today," Thomas said importantly. "I'm in charge!"

Spencer was worried.

"Oh my, Spencer," said Thomas. "You are a mess! I'll check you over from wheels to whistle! Put Spencer up on the hoist, please, Kevin!"

"Thank you, Kevin," Thomas said absently.
"Are you listening, Thomas?" asked Victor.
"Yes, Victor," said Thomas.

But Thomas was too excited to listen. He wanted to get on with his very important job!

"Don't worry. I know just what to do," he said.

"Very well, my friend," said Victor. "Good luck!"

And Victor steamed away. Thomas was now in charge!

Victor was waiting for Thomas at the Steamworks.

"Hello, my friend!" said Victor. "This is a big day for you! The Steamworks will be very busy."

"Not too busy for me, Victor!" said Thomas. "I like being busy."

"That's good, my friend," said Victor. "Now, when engines come in, you have to listen carefully to their problems. If you need help, ask Kevin."

"That's right, Thomas," said Kevin. "When you're in a fix, look no further. Just ask Kevin—it'll save you bother!"

One morning, Sir Topham Hatt had a new job for Thomas.

"Victor has to go to the Transfer Yards," Sir Topham Hatt told him. "He will be away all day. You must look after the Steamworks in his place. Victor will tell you all you need to know. Make sure you listen carefully!"

"Yes, sir!" peeped Thomas.

Random House New York

Thomas the Tank Engine & Friends™

CREATED BY BRITT ALLCROFT

Based on The Railway Series by The Reverend W Awdry.
© 2012 Gullane (Thomas) LLC.
Thomas the Tank Engine & Friends and Thomas & Friends are trademarks of Gullane (Thomas) Limited.
HIT and the HIT Entertainment logo are trademarks of HIT Entertainment Limited.
All rights reserved. Published in the United States by Random House Children's Books, a division of Random House, Inc.,
1745 Broadway, New York, NY 10019, and in Canada by Random House of Canada Limited, Toronto. Random House
and the colophon are registered trademarks of Random House, Inc.
randomhouse.com/kids   www.thomasandfriends.com
ISBN: 978-0-307-93119-1
MANUFACTURED IN CHINA   10 9 8 7 6 5 4 3 2 1